Foreboding and Circumstance in Ohio

Rough Cut

"And even he, this adept in sound sense, in spite of all his assumed and cheaply acquired wisdom, is not exempt from wandering inadvertently beyond objects of experience into the field of chimeras." – Immanuel Kant

Dedicated to GPS

Contents

Note on the Text

The following short story was written over four days. Spelling and Grammar mistakes are deliberate. Tense jumping is deliberate as well. I hope you can follow.

Foreboding and Circumstance in Ohio

A Gonzo-Stream of Consciousness-Existential-Post Modern Comedic Novella

What am I doing? I'm driving, but I don't know where I'm driving to. For the life of me I can't remember. Not only can I not remember where I'm going, but I can't remember for how long I haven't known where I'm going. Have the last few years been like this, my entire life? I suppose at a certain point I must have known where I was going because otherwise I wouldn't have a frame of reference to say I don't know where I'm going. Eventually one must pick a cutoff point, but where? Will I slip into infinite regress? How am I still driving? I can't remember even looking at the road the past few minutes. Who stopped at lights? Who didn't run over kids at crosswalks? Simply put, I don't know and in an odd way the fact that I don't know is reassuring. This drive feels like déjà vu, it all seems so familiar, as if there were no other outcomes that my actions could be taking right now. I feel deterministically trapped. The vivacious girl in the car next to me is texting on her cell phone. To my left an older gentleman is reading a pamphlet on the corner. He looks like an executive of a corporation, but one that was promoted from within, originating from the engineering department instead of an MBA program. How do they do it? How does the vivacious girl and the engineer looking executive go on living? I suppose either hedonic adaption has set in and colors their vision of the world. Or perhaps, they simple choose not to think about it. But what is it?

My retreat into my own thoughts is turning oppressive at the moment. All of the vital functions of a human being are being run completely by my subconscious. My optic vision, muscle movement, practical reasoning, and the cooperation of all succinctly utilized to drive this car are all being run by my subconscious to functional perfection. Have I found the highest form of yoga or transcendental meditation? Existing in this state is quite amazing really, if one thinks about it, which is not too hard given that that's all I am capable of at this point. In this state I drift away to a conversation I had with my parents the night before.

The actual words of what were said the night before are unimportant, for the essence derived from human experience adopted by the absolute experience of people has completely colored language and rendered them nondescriptive details. Specific constructions of words are rendered irrelevant by the essence of the conversation. And that essence is what creates the comfortable numb haze we all exist within. What is all that I have just said in this paragraph? I don't know, one cannot be sure of anything one says in this state, even that previous statement. But back to the unimportant words. My mother was saying something to the tune of, "It's just…….just…….you know…….He's just weird." And that was it. The debate was closed. Simple nice and neat. Which is emblematic of my mother. If I had to describe her in one sentence, a combination of Willy Loman and Dr. Pangloss shrouded in a cloak of benevolent hedonism comes to mind. I sat listening eating quietly. Other than eating, which I was doing subconsciously, I couldn't see if there was any point. I already had questioned whether I could discern a point or whether there was any point to discern at all. In my esoteric thought process all I knew was that they were missing the point. And by they, I mean everyone I encountered in life. It's as if, looking around at everyone, everyone was missing the point. I don't know what point they were missing, but everyone was missing it. That I knew. That much I knew. Everyone was existing in a world that was analogous to wearing an itchy sweater. As long as you kept your self distracted and didn't think about it, the the itchiness of the sweater didn't bother you and it kept you warm. As long as you didn't think about it, you were comfortably warm. But once you started to think about it, once you were self aware, the sweater became decidedly uncomfortable. I suppose the sweater is necessary to protect one from the cold, but thus one needs to distract oneself from the itchiness in order to survive. Perhaps this is why I'm in a constant state of discomfort all of the time. Why I feel so comfortably out of place.

This whirlwind of thought was cascading throughout my head as my parents droned on about the importance of getting a good job. But all I could think about was that it didn't matter. None of it mattered. Nothing mattered. Whether my subconscious could achieve through the application and interview process to earn a job, because I certainly wouldn't be conscious for that process, and then subconsciously worked at this new found job, it didn't matter. There would be no change in the world, there would be no change in my self. We would have another conversation and then another conversation about this same job topic again and again with my parents. But it didn't matter, either way, nothing would change. Perhaps I'm not intelligent enough or lacking in the basic mental fortitudes for acceptable self deception and mental compartmentalization. Without immense self deception and mental compartmentalization, how can one move on in an arbitrary universe? How does everyone else do it? What is it?

Instinctively I snap back to my present predicament. The car makes a right turn into the parking lot of La Fiesta the local Mexican restaurant. I was late, but late for me, not late in general. I'm almost always running late to everything; classes, engagements with friends, sexual experiences, conscious conversations, so suffice to say, I think people expect me to be late in general, which explains a lot, I think. One can never be sure of these things, especially one's esoteric thoughts. Again I've drifted off, I don't know how I've gotten to the door. Somewhere along the line I've parked the car, gotten out and walked across the parking lot with numerous insignificant obstacles to navigate, people and cars mostly, and am now standing in the lobby and apparently talked to the host who is directing me to my friends table. I'm 20 minutes late to join them, which is rude for me or at least what I feel is rude, but even more rude because the service here at La Fiesta is demonstratively efficient. Your chips and salsa arrive within mere seconds, probably less than 10. Your food within 15, but mostly more like 12 minutes. La Fiesta may not look like much from the outside driving by, but it is a classic affirmation of everything that is good and decent in the world all rolled up into a tortilla sprinkled with MSG. If I will find salvation anywhere it will be in here.

I apologize to my friends and we begin talking uneristially. The conversation generally revolves around independent comments designed for immediate limited humor whose point of origin originated somewhere in our past surrounding high school or university. I start to ease back into that state of active relative contemporary unconscious rumination I spend most of my time in. How do other people avoid this state? It doesn't matter, but how do they avoid it? It doesn't matter. My three friends were all sitting around the table talking and eating their food.

I look around without moving my head and view my friends. Apparently I have laughed at something my friend Ryan has said. I didn't intend to notice. I don't really intend to do anything, they just arbitrarily happen. Outside of my control. They could just as well happen to someone else as me. It doesn't really matter. Perhaps Ryan having a kid just happened. Seems about as likely as anything else. Others with greater ability to consciously selectively think might say it would be an overstatement to say that he didn't intend to have a child. It's doesn't matter, it happened. Ryan was 'trapped' here in our high school hometown to be near his kid's mother who was a few years younger than us and who did not attend university. Their having a child was an unexpected surprise, an unknowable unknown. Ryan had had to transfer to another university closer to our home in order to help raise his child. The worst part was it wasn't even his. Each one of us knew she cheated on him. But how do you tell your friend to get a paternity test? I mean it's too late now, he's attached to it. It doesn't matter anyway. So anyway, Ryan was stuck with his daughter, which it seems he has tricked himself into believing was a significant event in his life. I don't see how anyone could make that determination, but it confines the way he lives his life. But more than that, it gave him an excuse for his mediocrity, his dreams he was never going to achieve anyway. Now he had an out, a universal catchphrase he could employ in virtually any situation, which he lorded over others. If only everyone else had such an excuse, more things would get done in the world. It's an odd phenomenon. As you may have already guessed, I don't know what I'm doing or more importantly why I'm doing anything I'm doing, or still more important yet, why I think that why I do anything is important. Yet I can make value judgments about society and people. Maybe you do not need to understand something to play. And maybe the rules of chess aren't really the rules of chess, and people who think they've won have really lost or tied or both or won. Everyone is guessing about the rules, which makes them arbitrary, and thus they don't matter. Whatever it is, I don't know what it is or at least I don't know that I know what it is. If you've kept reading up until now, congratulations. All you need to know is that Ryan has a kid and it is keeping him here in our hometown, to be near the mother, and preventing him from achieving his dreams. Ryan has a kid. And all that that entails. And I suppose in his own way Ryan felt trapped too. Unlike me, he didn't have the luxury of retreating into himself. While I didn't think his child was important, he did. His daughter mattered to him and thus he felt trapped by the obligations he placed on himself.

Our conversation had drifted toward Ryan complaining about his job at a local pizza establishment. The first to comment was Chris. Chris had been quite the athlete in junior high.

Superb sprinter and football player. His parents were relatively wealthy for the area, but not actually wealthy on a national basis. They were victims of their regional and lower middle class attitudes toward wealth and education. They knew enough to work within the system, but not enough to really understand the economic system we all live and operate within. If, in their established years, they had learned to understand how the economic system worked, it would have been too late for them to change career paths. There is only so high a doctor and day trader can climb economically if they are uncreative and not particularly clever. Degrees hanging on a wall can only take you so far on their own. If they had known exactly which fields to enter they could have obtained all that they sought. They threw lavish parties with three live bands at their home, but charged money to enter, not because it was a bourgeois snub at traditional etiquette signifying they were on a certain faint level above the rules, but they charged money because they needed it to pay for their party. While their efforts scandalized the local social scenes, they would have been thoroughly outclassed in certain circles in New York, not simply outclassed, but priced out. Simply put they didn't earn enough money, which created a disequilibrium. Their aspirations were much higher than their means. Inside the void of nothingness created by this disequilibrium was the environment in which Chris was raised. He had everything materially one could want, but guidance. His parents were more concerned with social circles than his upbringing. They didn't do all of the typical parental duties indulging his interests and teaching him a basic sense of Judeo-Christian right and wrong. All of that provides a filter of distractions that keeps people enslaved with the false notion that they understand how the world works. In a way Chris was trapped in his parents' circumstances conflated into him. He wasn't protected from the absurdity of the world at a young age like most. He confronted absurdity head on, but like a toddler in a university class, he didn't have the means to interact with absurdity or to even process what he was encountering. He'd opened his eyes before they were able to handle sunlight. Walking around simultaneously mesmerized and terrified of the amorphous blobs of light that comprised his vision of the world, like trying to find your way out of kaleidoscope. Everyone says his drug use was attributed to his parents' lack of attention and their poor upbringing. But I think he turned to drugs to cope with the absurdity of the world, to try and make sense of the kaleidoscope of the world he couldn't interpret or interact with, or maybe he was trying to numb his senses. It must have been a tough thing for him to realize at an early age that there was no point, no end goal to life. That where you started from didn't matter either. That nothing is permanent, everything is in a constant state of flux and change and each change or flux doesn't matter, doesn't connect to anything else. That life is to be lived in the flux with that constant feeling of being out on a limb, and you better get used to it, because it's not going anywhere. That kind of absurdity is impossible to reconcile (I mean have you been reading this book so far?), but painful if you don't even know what you're looking at, like the toddler at university staring at a calculus problem. Chris has come face to face with absurdity and found a way to keep living, or maybe he was too much of a coward to kill himself. Either way he kept on living. His drug use had nearly kept him out of university. He was really quite lucky to have gotten into Ohio University, which in hindsight was the worst thing for him if the goal was to reduce or maintain his drug use. For those of you who do not know about Ohio University, it is the first university established west of the Appalachian Mountains. Nestled in Athens, Ohio, a hippie college town. Compared to the much more highly ranked university I attended, I would describe the girls at Ohio University as twice as hot and twice as dumb. I was the only one of the four of us who had not attended Ohio University. The academic reputation of the school could be summed up in t-shirts sold throughout the town which proclaimed Ohio University as 'the best five or six years of your life.' Combine the social and academic aspects with the liberal hippie culture of Athens and the university in general; the end result was an easy good time, a very easy time. As you may have surmised with where I'm heading with this, drugs were even more available at Ohio University than in our town. For someone who never really could comprehend the absurdity of life, university was the tipping point for Chris. He crashed out after two years, barely completing a year of academic credit in the process and spent the next four years in rehab facilities from California to Ohio. He was clean now, but barely holding on. Kind of like a British colony made up of a mix of disparate peoples who had no business associating with each other in any context, but who were firmly united together in the face of the evil British colonizers. Once the British left, even the ever so slightest hint of conflict would send the new country into civil war. He looked as though things could fall apart at any minute, and like the British leaving their former colonies, everyone knew it was going to happen and probably happen soon, but no one knew exactly when. At the end of the day, Chris was a man searching for religion. He needed something to believe in, but something off the shelf to believe in. He had to get it lock stock and barrel. The knowledge to interact with the absurdity of the world he did not possess, and thus he couldn't create his own religion to use. So Chris was constantly spinning, grasping onto anything without the ability to discern that nothing in the world mattered, all of this in a world that didn't matter. Most people would call that absurd, but I thought it was logical.

Wow these last few paragraphs have been prescient and probably quite pretentious. How was I able to string these coherent thoughts and judgments together, especially when I don't think there is any merit to making judgments of any kind? I suppose it will make this story comprehensible, which implies a desire for you the reader to understand what I'm saying. Or maybe it is just an attempt to make this story less esoteric.

The last of my friends at the table is John. John is a man who likes to think of himself as embracing the absurdity of life and living his own Nieztchean will to power lifestyle as best as polite white society will allow him, or he will allow himself. In reality his lifestyle is pure hedonism. He isn't a believer or really a thinker, he is living his Nieztchean outlook because it is counter culture, it is cool, it is different than the main stream. Which seems like a dumb reason to like something. Defining yourself in opposition to something still means you are defining yourself by that something, you are just defining yourself differently in terms of relation to that something. I don't hold any of that against John or criticize him at all. It doesn't matter how one lives one's life. But that is the way John is. He is one of the few who are the most hopelessly enslaved because they falsely think they are free. He is enslaved to the same way of thinking he thought he escaping from and thought he was free from. He has rebelled right back to his jail cell. Maybe he realized that and maybe that is why he seemed to have angst in his actions. Anyway John is up for just about anything and anyone. He is a hedonistically predictable wild card. He will say something predictably off-the-wall to add to the conversation. It keeps things exciting until hedonic adaptation sets in. The mere fact I can sit and analyze his conversational behavior means I have adapted and am bored by it. I think he worried the same, perhaps that is why he is so defensive about himself. Don't ever steer the conversation towards him in even a remotely jokingly critical manor, that's a conversation killer for John. All in all, he's more fun than the average guy to have around. In our youth he used to through rocks at parked cars. And that was fine by me. It didn't change me, it simply didn't matter, like all the other details about people's lives, they don't matter.

I didn't notice the food I was eating during this series of conversations with my three friends. For a while now I haven't really noticed food. Food was something I needed to keep on living and that was really all it was. I didn't really pay any attention to what I was eating because five minutes later it wouldn't make a difference. I wouldn't be important, it wasn't important, and it isn't important now. I just didn't see any differentiating points of any substance anymore.

After our very efficient and timely meal was coming to a conclusion, John suggested we join Lawrence, who was having a bit of a get together, in his garage to smoke. Lawrence is a jazz guitarist and a very good one too. He'd won a scholarship to the most prestigious university for music out east. Playing the jazz guitar gave Lawrence purpose, a driving purpose, the kind of purpose that makes one happy to block out everything else in life. Lawrence knew exactly what he wanted out of life and exactly what he wanted to do in life. He had the ultimate lifelong distraction, purpose. I can't describe how envious of Lawrence's purpose I am. I don't think playing the jazz guitar matters any more than Oscar the Grouch playing the lids of garbage cans or eating peanut butter for that matter, but Lawrence has a tremendous power of self-delusion which has its uses in the world we live in. If he wanted he could flip back in forth between realities or at the very least give himself a respite from the world. Lawrence had been a friend of ours in high school as well. He was back home to visit his family. We decided to drive to his house.

Lawrence's garage looks like any other garage one happens upon in life, except that the back left corner is divided from ceiling to floor with blue tarp that made a smaller room. Inside this blue tarp room are welding equipment, a worktable, three or four folding chairs, and a cooler. John, Chris, and Ryan's favorite activity to do when Lawrence is in town is go to his blue tarp garage room and smoke. On this particular occasion two girls had also joined us as well. Lawrence kept his smoking paraphernalia under a frisbee on the work table. As we sat and talked our conversation never deviated in essence from our conversation at La Fiesta, every conversation point originated in the past and revolved around high school and university. It was mostly a lot of remising about university years and how they were better than the time we were having now.

John was remarking about how he used to be able to walk to Chirs' house near the university and hangout/smoke at 2 in the afternoon. Since he has a job now, he is prevented from doing that, and apparently that really sucks, life will never be that good or free again. What they really mean is that they can't trick themselves out of societal responsibility anymore. Their deferred responsibility has come to an end and it has really kicked them hard. They are now meekly vocally ignorantly lashing out at the perceived loss of innocence infecting the people around them. I thought the whole thing was a boring exercise in polite futility. There weren't any differences between university and now, nothing mattered. They never had innocence, only the illusion of innocence. The only difference was that their ignorance was gone. Why am I the only one who thinks and sees that? They were clearly missing it. But what was it? Maybe they weren't missing it and I since I didn't know or couldn't identify what it is, they were right on it, I just couldn't tell.

Not terribly long ago I talked like them. I remember those days, not too long ago, a few months ago in fact. This is what I talked about, what I talked like. What I complained about. I fiercely lamented the loss of the perceived freedom of my university years. I fiercely didn't want to come to terms with it. But at a certain point it became an absurdity. It was in the past, which I couldn't change and which didn't matter anymore, so it was an exercise in the absurd to dwell on something that didn't have any meaning and didn't matter.

At a certain point the reminiscing reaches a fever pitch and it morphs into actionable nostalgia. Chris, John, and Ryan become blissfully aware that they have cars, weren't living in a military dictatorship, and that Athens, Ohio and Ohio University are a mere two hour drive away. We all decided to leave the first thing the next morning, a Saturday, for Athens and Ohio University.

I was a bit hazy in the car during the early morning hours when we began our drive. That beautiful time when you're awake but not really aware and everything passing by out the window seems to have a golden haze around it. The kind of state where starring out the window you passively daydream even though there are other people around you and they are talking and having conversations. That state makes living possible.

The car casually rolls across the southern Ohio hills like a rolling stone, without a care in the world. The euphoria of the coming weekend was kicking in. Kind of like a drug, temporarily taking one back to a state. And like a drug, it was pure escapism. We were temporarily escaping from our currently reality. This trip wasn't really about the weekend or about nostalgia, it was about escape. Our revolt the night before, just like every other youth revolt in history was about escape. But what were we really escaping from? And where were we really escaping from? I didn't know. I sat back and started daydreaming about something else as I looked out the window content in the knowledge that it didn't matter.

About five minutes before entering Athens one finds several historical signs indicating relevant historical information about the town, each sign nestled among the scenic green hills of the

Hocking. Entering Athens we drove past rows of motorcycles, about 60 in my estimation, and a few biker bars frequented by the local townies. We then rolled into the inner town with its shops, hippie vegan co-ops, bars, diners, t-shirt shops, and at the end the university. The closer we rolled towards the university the more electric the car became, the more enthused and riled up the group became. Compared to the night before, this was a tremendous opportunity and we were out for blood.

Our stone finally came to a stop at a single level home occupied by two of John's previous roommates about two blocks away from downtown Athens, down the street from the university, and across the street from a rather drab three story warehouse. About fourteen pairs of shoes had been through over and hung from the phone lines above the street of the single level house. Both of John's previous roommates were on the five or six year Ohio University graduation plan. Still living the dream. John had graduated in four years a tremendous accomplishment everyone kept telling me. It suited our immediate needs.

After we had gotten settled and broken out the Jack one of John's friends came over. Her name was Kay. Kay was a girl of average height with brown hair and a nonchalantly inquisitive demeanor. Marginally above average in general with a streak of reclus abandon tamed with a lack of self-confidence, but intelligent nonetheless. She was a few years younger than John and she was a senior this year. She and John had hooked up sporadically several times while John was at university and on all of John's subsequent visits. John was fully expecting to hook up with her again tonight. Perhaps she was a physical connection to John's university years, maybe, but it was probably about sex. At a certain point as the sun was going down, we, that is myself and Kay, were left alone on the porch of the house. I asked her about her interest in psychology and her desire to pursue a master's degree but not a Phd, too much work apparently, I couldn't really see the difference. She asked me where I went to school and I told her. She remarked that I went to a good school. I shrugged and said it didn't matter. It didn't matter. She didn't look perplexed or turned off by my remark like most people, every person I had encountered. Perhaps it was her inquisitive nature that kept her cool or interested, but for the first time I was intrigued. It didn't matter, but yet I couldn't help being intrigued.

It was the time of night to head out, so we set out. We were walking to a house party in the house of one of Chris and John's friends Ian. I would later find out after the fact that Ian was studying to be a botanist, which was more common than one would think at this university. Ian's house was pretty large as far as college houses go. There were at least 150 people at his house. Ian and his housemates had constructed a large fire pit in the backyard that everyone was drinking and worshipping around. The house was on a hill and the backyard ended in a steep cliff like drop over a gulch. People were throwing empty bottles and cans at people and cars across from the gulch in addition to urinating off the side. Mellow stoner music was blasting up to a volume highly inappropriate for any kind of serious smoking, only background smoking. All in all people seemed to be really enjoying themselves. John, Ryan, and Chris all seemed to be having a good time. All manner of whimsical party charades were happening all around the fire complete with people having sex in several areas in and around the house with only a slight touch of addition privacy than would be afforded close to the fire. Then, I'm not sure if it was the bottle throwing, the fire, or the music, but the police stormed the party in force.

Apparently the police had to deal with riots quite frequently in Athens and they often found themselves outnumbered by agitated, drunk college students, which probably explains why they showed up in force and prepared for a conflict. Initially I stood back and admired the show through the fire. The sight of black clad police officers pillaging the party goers through the dancing flames of the fire was entertaining, and if I had been someone else I would probably have described the view through the dancing flames as lovely. The mellow stoner music provided a surreal backdrop in which the events seemed to happen in slow motion. Each strike of a person with a club was set to mellow guitar music. It was art really. I sat still, motionless, entertained as police officers in riot gear beat members of the party seemingly at random. Even though everything around me was in chaos, I was at peace, content. Perhaps the police had had enough of the university students abusing them over the years or, probably correctly, had deduced the drunken, agitated general state of the party and decided their only chance at a resolution would be to deal a death blow first, either way, they struck pugnaciously hard. Part of the terror of the police that night was the seemingly arbitrary way they picked recipients of their blows. If it had been orderly and calculated people would not have been afraid psychologically as much, still physically intimidated, but not psychologically afraid. One cannot plan for random. When there is no discernable reason for actions, they are unpredictable, and everyone believes that they can be a victim. It's the fear of the unknown. I never understood why terrorists went after political and well established targets. Everyone knows they are going to target them, making them easier to defend, and they make their attacks easy to isolate yourself from for the vast majority of the population. If they were smart they would attack random malls in medium sized suburban towns across the country, all picked at random. That would really scare people. People are most of afraid of the dark, of the unknown, of the random. I've slipped into that state again. I am observing and commenting on what I see around me. My subconscious is controlling all my physical movements, which leaves me free to watch a cop and his eyes scan the crowd, his eyes moving over kid after kid after kid after kid after kid until he stops and zeroes in on his prize, John. They both run each set of legs moving through the dancing flames of the great bonfire. A guitar solo plays in the background fittingly. The police officer is not faster than John, but the police officer is also not drunk. He catches John out of a crowd of 25 or more, pushing aside other members just to get to John. He could have hit 20 or so kids by now, but he is locked in John, which must be scary for John, because he doesn't know why he has been picked. But with one big roar of the fire's flames the police officer catches John and smashes him across the face. He then gives John a fierce upper cut with the butt of his club. The blood on John's face reflects a bit of light and image of the fire in it. Why is this what I notice in this moment?

I'm not really sure what happened. As I've been describing all of this I have somehow helped Ryan and Chis drag John out of the botanist's house and onto the street. I can't remember doing any of it. I look down and John is moaning on the pavement and Ryan and Chris are yelling about how unfair the police are by nature and how unfair they have just acted. I told them we need to get John to hospital to attend to his head injuries. They agree. They keep going on about what just happened with the police, which I find to be silly speculation. It doesn't matter I told them. They stare abjectly at me and ask me what I meant. I tell them again that what just occurred didn't matter. That what happened to John. It didn't matter. What's the matter with you was their response. I couldn't see how it mattered.

I left Ryan and Chris at the emergency room with John. They were too shaken up to continue going out. They kept postulating the same premise about the fundamentally evil nature of the police. They were angry that I wanted to keep going out. The night was still quite young; it was only a short duration past midnight. I felt the same as I had during the attack, why not go out again. So I left for the main street with its bars.

The bar scene was uneventful and of no importance. When I was finished it was a bit past three in the morning and I decided to walk back to the house we were staying in.

When I was about two blocks away from the house I noticed four guys walking towards me. I didn't think anything of them until we got a bit closer. They were all clearly drunk, but not sloppy drunk, an angry aggressive drunk. On any given night multiple people are like that. Nothing changed at all in their demeanor as I walked past them. I wasn't able to tell with any certainty, but I doubt their demeanor changed when one stuck me in the back of the head. I fell to the ground as they kicked me. The one who had been walking in the front of their group then proceeded to punch me in ribs the five times. As surprising fast as the incident had started, I watched them walk away from my position rolling on the ground. They walked away as if nothing had happened. Their walk and demeanor were the same as before we encountered each other. The only change, the only difference lay with my wheezing on the sidewalk. There was no reason for picking me, there never is. Really the only thing of note from this random beating I had endured was the fact that I had not entered that contemplative state where my subconscious controls my movements. Perhaps it happened to fast, I'm not sure. But it was out of the ordinary. For me.

I had recovered enough to stand up. A guy about my age ran over to me to ask if I was ok and if there was anything he could do. I said it didn't matter. He asked if I needed to go to the hospital and if I knew the guys who had attached me. All of his questions didn't matter. He was all of these questions that didn't matter. Why was he so concerned? Why was I not concerned? Could I even tell if I was concerned? In any effect, I proceeded to beat this good Samaritan up. Up implies a bit of a positive connotation, when in fact there was no connotation. I hit him several times in the face and chest, I then kneed him in the stomach and finally the head. He dropped unconscious onto the sidewalk. Where was there any connotation in that? I can't find any. I opened his wallet and took the 27 dollars in his wallet. Again I didn't slip into that contemplative state. I was fully aware of everything.

Walking away down the street towards the house I was staying in I knew my friends would ask me about happened. I would say it didn't matter. Why did I do the things I just did? No reason. I didn't need the money from that good Samaritan. It didn't matter.

The only aspect I couldn't shake was my head. That blow I had suffered to the back of my head still caused me discomfort. I was changed by the incident, my head hurt. That I did know, and at the moment, it was an important consideration of mine.

Once I reached the house, I decided to go to the warehouse across the street. I didn't feel like sleeping and my head hurt too much to engage in conversation with anyone. Reaching the top of the warehouse was surprising easy. The door had been wedged open and I took the stairs once inside. Perhaps others had the same thought I did.

It was a warm Ohio summer night on the roof of the warehouse. I looked out across the university and the town. They were still vibrant. People were walking home and about. I walked right up to the edge of the roof so that my toes were almost off the edge. I stood up strait and put my arms strait out of my body at 90 degree angles and closed my eyes. I find myself routinely performing this exercise. Because when you are alone and standing on the edge of a cliff or a sufficiently tall building you are confronted with total freedom and the rush of the feeling of total freedom. The decision to jump or not to jump is completely yours. Societal restrictions, other people, and all the countless influences that cage a person's behavior in the world don't apply to that decision. It is entirely yours to jump or not to jump. Many people stand on the edge of a cliff and feel that rush, that ecstasy of total freedom and are scarred by it. Perhaps the novelty of it scares them. A person so rarely, perhaps never, experiences total freedom. If a person is having a conversation with someone in a café there are so many restrictions placed upon that person, most are absorbed and applied subconsciously. That person regulates the volume of their voice, the content of their language, what they are wearing, and so on, these little things add up, and that person gets use to it, to the point that they don't notice. They first learnt to live with then they learn to find security in their chains because their chains have become familiar, safe. That's why they are scarred by total freedom; it's a different way of life. I've been using these cliff top freedom sessions as a drug if I'm being honest with myself. It's the only decision, that if I'm being completely honest with myself, matters, it is the only one that interests me. I care whether I jump or not.

While I was standing on the edge of the warehouse I heard footsteps carefully approaching foot by foot. I turned around and saw Kay slowly walking towards me. She didn't say anything, she just kept slowly and methodically walking towards me. By the moment she stopped right in front of me I had stepped back down from the ledge of the warehouse. We looked at each other for what seemed like fifteen minutes but in actuality was probably only fifteen seconds. While starring into my eyes without blinking she asked what I was doing. I responded without blinking that I was experiencing freedom. Neither of us said anything further for what was probably another fifteen seconds. I then brushed a hair back from the side of her face and kissed her. I knew John would be upset since he wanted to sleep with her. But I didn't care. In that moment I wanted to be with her and being with her was important to me.

I was completely conscious while we were having sex. I noticed and enjoyed everything. Until she started to reach orgasm. It seemed like a wave came up and over her starting in her feet and working up to her eyes. She closed her eyes and retreated into herself. Completely into herself, until she was alone with her pleasure. I was left all alone. It was an odd phenomenon that I hadn't noticed before. I was physically inside another human being, I was as close as I would ever be to another human being, and yet, I was utterly and completely alone. Not only was I alone, but I was further away from her than I had ever been from a person. This wasn't a shared experience, sex, despite physically being inside another human being, it wasn't a shared experience. No pleasure would come from her, I had to create it for myself. In this experience I had to give it meaning, I had to make it real to me, no one could do that other than me. I had to make experience real to me, I had to give experience meaning.

I didn't sleep that night. A calm had descended over me, a relaxing calm that comes from understanding. I sat out on the ledge of the warehouse and watched the sun come up. The sun coming up didn't matter to the world or anyone else, but it mattered to me in that moment. It didn't have any meaning in and of itself, but it did have meaning to me, because I gave it meaning, because it mattered to me. Within that esoteric microcosm of my mind, it had meaning, and since I was the only one who mattered, it had meaning, singular but meaning. It was the first experience watching the sun rise that I consciously enjoyed.

I went to get breakfast. I walked over the spot I had been attacked and the spot I had attacked that Samaritan. As I got closer to town the streets became crowded. I keep walking looking at the sunrise getting thicker and thicker in the sea of people until I was completely consumed and lost in the crowd, indistinguishable from anyone else in the crowd from a distance.

The End

Selected Poems

Choosing

east or west. One must choose

The middle sun revels up high

Burning tears of sweat past the

Brow which shelters blue Eyes

Who witness the death of

Day and night in their sea

Trapped by choice

the blackness hides the night

One trying, Illuminating, Demanding

Straining eyes, uncertain of the

Interpretation of the land

illuminated by the creeping light

Inspiration and precarious

The morning sun wants one

As long as one is prepared to work

It will follow, but may leave

As quickly as lightning, a soggy departure

Is it worth it?

The relaxing cool colors of evening

Demand nothing more than your gaze

lids close on the twin blue seas

The subconscious works

The contenting western colors reside within

But upon the eastern beams brings the uncomfortable, tiring factory of realization

A tightrope of creative destruction

No trail of lost hair in the west

only accepting beauty, and night's

Blackness erases all

Reinventing justification or Unconditional acceptance?

All Men

All men kill, ,what they love

All men kill, ,what they love

All men kill, ,what they love

Like Sisyphus and his boulder,

The weight is constant, without

Escape. From ever watching collective eyes, we toil

Shaped by the whims and desires of popular sentiment

To the cracked sidewalk of daily life

Innocence gives way to empathy

Neither will help a man

Suffocating him into survival

As the collective eyes watch,

Him give up to survive

Give up what built him into a human

For a glimpse of what it means to be human -

In the collective eyes

They ask only for acceptance

The punishment for condemnation is

Isolation and lonely freedom

Acceptance is to smother with the eyes watching

Ever watching, ever watching

Waiting for the sacrifice of man's humanity

We see it unfold

Each pixel of an eye is us

We stare down collectively

Bound by those same collective eyes

As we push our boulder up the hill

With his boulder Sisyphus laughs

He laughs at u headed warnings

All men kill, ,what they love

All men kill, ,what they love

All men kill, ,what they love

Old Country

Fleeing from Turks

Another Greek tragedy

The chorus sings from across the sea

Rome has fallen, but the seven hills remain

From farms to Worchester street

Nothing more than another ocean

Hope for prosperity put on layaway

Exiles in spirit

Only a matter of time before the chorus

Echoes through time

The seven hills remain

Circumstances

I get in my car and drive

Nowhere in particular

Ah, now I remember

To meet friends at the restaurant

Why am I going? I can't for the life of me remember why

What has happened?

In high school and college it was easy

This thing called life

Why do I do what I do now?

We all leave life the same way we came in

Where is the ever present exuberance to get lost in

It was so easy

I use to think these thoughts

Deriving no small degree of consternation

That tortured and ruled my conscious

The world was so, until

I had sex with a girl in Athens

Not the first time I had sex

But the first time it meant something

At a certain point, her eyes rolled back and closed

She was in that toe curly ecstasy

A wave crashing over her

Her eyes closed, and she retreated inside herself with the pleasure

I was utterly alone

Physically inside someone, but alone

More alone then I ever had before

Or would be in my life

Not even sex, being as close as I could be to someone

Could create that overbearing exuberance

I would have to create my own

No circumstances could produce real happiness

The responsibility was mine

I don't know why sex was the straw

But it was

That was the day I grew up

Seeing Blind

the wind whips my cheeks

Stinging, an alert redness that

Opens and focuses my eyes

Whistling along the brick and past

A streetlamp, which sheds light

And allows me to see. To see

A blind women. Who really sees

She knows not the color

Of the streetlamp's projections

Only of its warmth and that it is

No matter what color the brick

Inhabits. A mere distraction.

It keeps here safe from the

Whipping wind. So cold

On her face. A reddish hugh

On the cheeks of the one

Who really sees. Sees

All of us, for who we really

Are, the blinded. For

The streetlamp is our curse.

Looking into the all-seeing

Eyes of the blind women.

Who really sees

Fernando Giannotti is a writer and economist from Dayton, Ohio. He is a member of the comedy troupe '5 Barely Employable Guys.' He holds a B.A. in economics and history and an M.S. in finance from Vanderbilt University. A self-labeled doctor of cryptozoology, he continues to live the gonzo-transcendentalist lifestyle and strives to live an examined life.